Greta's Leash

MEL JONES

AuthorHouse™
1663 Liberty Drive
Bloomington, IN 47403
www.authorhouse.com
Phone: 833-262-8899

This book is printed on acid-free paper.

ISBN: 979-8-8230-0320-9 (sc)
ISBN: 979-8-8230-0316-2 (e)

Library of Congress Control Number: 2023904505

Print information available on the last page.

Published by AuthorHouse 03/18/2023

authorHOUSE®

Greta's Leash

Author and Illustrator: Mel Jones

This is Greta! She is an awesome and wonderful dog, and an important member of the Jones family! Greta loves going for long walks with her girl Kaitie, spending time with her family and being outside exploring!

Her family also loves being outside, and they spend lots of time at Grandpa Jones' woods. They go there for family get-togethers, to picnic and to fish in the pond. One Saturday Kaitie's family decided to load up their truck and go fishing. Kaitie asked her dad, "Can Greta go too?!" "Only if you keep her on her leash," said Dad. "I will!" said Kaitie.

Kaitie's family had been fishing for only a little while when Kaitie said, "I'm bored, can I take Greta for a walk?" "Only if you are careful and keep her on her leash," said Mom. "I will," said Kaitie. "I promise!".

Kaitie grabbed Greta's leash. "C'mon girl,
let's go!", and away they went to start a
new adventure deep in the woods.

Now Greta had a very special leash that could be made longer with just a click of a button, which made exploring much more fun! She loved sniffing everyone and everything around her.

They had not gone far when Greta noticed a strange creature. She stretched her leash to get a closer look. Kaitie shouted, “Be careful Greta, that is a praying mantis!” Greta didn’t listen and all of a sudden the bug raised up his spiky front legs and grabbed Greta’s nose! “YIP!”, yelled Greta.

Greta tossed her head and shook the praying mantis off her nose. However, the bug got stuck in her leash and couldn't get free. This didn't end Greta and Kaitie's walk. Kaitie just made Greta's leash longer, and they kept on exploring.

Greta's hearing was just as strong as her sense of smell. As they were walking she heard a loud crunching noise. "Crunch, Crunch, Crunch!" Then she saw it! A big squirrel with his cheeks full of acorns was sitting next to a big oak tree. The squirrel didn't even notice Kaitie and Greta getting closer and closer. When he finally saw them, he jumped up and got tangled in Greta's leash!

Now there was a praying mantis and a squirrel stuck in Greta's leash! This didn't end Greta and Kaitie's walk. Kaitie just made Greta's leash longer, and kept on exploring.

Kaitie and Greta walked a little further and came to a small bridge going across the creek. They decided to go see what was on the other side. They were about halfway when Greta spied something hanging from the bottom of the bridge. Greta leaned way over the edge of the bridge to get a better look. She couldn't believe what she was seeing, and neither could Kaitie. "Shhhh Greta, be very quiet, so you don't wake the bat!" whispered Kaitie.

The little brown bat did wake up when he heard Greta's sniffing, but he didn't use his echolocation to know just how close Greta was to him. The little bat got confused and flapped right into Greta's leash! His feet were so tangled up that he couldn't get free. Now there was a praying mantis, squirrel and brown bat stuck in Greta's leash, but this didn't end Kaitie and Greta's walk. Kaitie just made the leash longer, and kept on exploring.

As soon as Kaitie and Greta had crossed the bridge they noticed a raccoon sitting on the bank of the creek getting ready to eat a crawdad that she had caught for her lunch. She did not notice Greta coming closer to get a better look until it was too late! The raccoon jumped up, and when she did, the crawdad pinched her paw. She was in so much pain that she just started running and got tangled in Greta's leash! The crawdad was still attached to her paw, so he was stuck too.

Kaitie was really enjoying the nature walk she and Greta were on, but even she was a little surprised by the raccoon and her "lunch" being tangled in the leash. She counted them, "1,2,3,4,5 Wow, 5 animals!" Then she thought, "I wonder how many more creatures are out there?" Sooo, she clicked the button on Greta's leash to make it longer and kept on exploring.

Now Kaitie and Greta had been walking for quite a while and their legs were getting tired, so they decided to stop and rest for a little bit. As they were sitting there they noticed a hole in the ground. In the hole they saw something pink, and they also noticed that the pink thing was moving. Greta went to get a closer look. As she was sniffing, a starred nosed mole popped up and then went back in. The mole did this several times. Greta was getting so excited about this funny little thing popping in and out that she started running around the hole as fast as she could! Kaitie was laughing so hard, "Oh, Greta, you are so silly!" Then Greta barked, and the mole came out of the hole too far and got tangled in the leash. The mole was yanked right out of the hole! "POP!"

Now there was a praying mantis, squirrel, brown bat, raccoon, crawdad and star nosed mole tangled in Greta's leash, and since they were rested, Kaitie made the leash longer and kept on exploring.

Kaitie was so excited when she saw flowers in the meadow up ahead. She couldn't wait to enjoy their sweet smell and pick some for her mom. Greta saw something totally different and it didn't smell like flowers. There was a new little black and white creature enjoying the scent of the meadow flowers and didn't see Greta coming up from behind. Greta started growling as she got closer

Then it happened!!! The small creature, which was a skunk, raised his tail and sprayed his special scent all over Greta's face! Greta was shocked and her eyes started watering from the stink. She took off without being able to see and ran right into the skunk. The skunk flew up into the air and then got tangled in Greta's leash!

Now there was a praying mantis, squirrel, brown bat, raccoon, crawdad, star nosed mole and a skunk tangled in Greta's leash! It was a little stinky, but Kaitie just clicked the button, the leash got longer, and they kept on exploring.

After running into a skunk, Kaitie thought it might be a good idea to start heading towards the pond and her family, but Greta had another idea. She was barking at a fox sitting next to a big hollow log, and before Kaitie knew it, the fox, Greta, the 7 extra animals and even Kaitie went into the log! It was a tight fit. There was a lot of commotion, and when they tumbled out the fox was also tangled in the leash!

Now there was a praying mantis, squirrel, brown bat, raccoon, crawdad, star nosed mole, skunk and a fox tangled in Greta's leash! Kaitie looked at Greta and said, "Girl, it's time to go back to the pond. Your leash is full of animals and there is no more room!"

Kaitie and Greta were just a little ways from the pond when Greta spied an opossum hanging upside down from a limb of a tree. She barked so loud that the little animal jumped from the limb and played dead so that Greta wouldn't eat her! However, something got to the opossum before Greta did! A turkey vulture who eats dead animals swooped down to get his lunch!

Since the opossum was only pretending to be dead, she grabbed the leash and held on tight so that the turkey vulture wouldn't fly away with her. The turkey vulture kept jerking and jerking to get the opossum to let go!

The vulture gave one more powerful jerk and all of the animals that had been stuck in the leash came loose and went flying through the air! When they all landed, they scurried away back into the woods. Kaitie made Greta's leash short again and headed to the pond and her family.

Kaitie and Greta walked up to their family who was ready to go home. When they saw them, Kaitie's dad said, "It was getting late, and we were starting to get worried about you two." Mom said, "What in the world have you two been doing all day?" Kaitie smiled and said, "Oh, we just went for a little walk."

FUN FACTS

Praying Mantis
A praying mantis can range from the size of a human fingernail to as big as a human forearm. It has 5 eyes, 2 compound and 3 simple and 1 ear on its stomach.

Squirrel
A squirrel has front teeth that never stop growing. It can find buried food beneath a foot of snow. A squirrel uses its tail for balance and as a parachute.

Brown Bat
A brown bat has a belly button. It can eat 1,000 insects in one night. A bat can reach speeds over 100 miles per hour.

Raccoon
A raccoon can see green, but no other colors. A raccoon was given to president Calvin Coolidge to eat for Thanksgiving, but he kept it for a pet instead. Raccoons that live in the city are smarter than raccoons that live in the country.

Crawdad
A crawdad swims backwards to avoid danger. It molts and then eats its own skeleton. A crawdad can regenerate lost limbs.

Star Nosed Mole
A star nosed mole can smell underwater. It can eat faster than any other mammal on earth. It has a tail that swells up 4 times larger with fat during winter.

Skunk
A skunk is immune to venom and can eat poisonous snakes. It does handstands to warn predators before spraying. It can shoot its stinky smell up to 10 feet.

Fox
A fox grins when it's afraid. It has supersonic hearing and can hear a watch ticking from 40 yards away. A fox uses the earth's magnetic field to hunt for food

Possum
An opossum has a super power of being immune to venom. She is pregnant for only 13 days. An opossum has 50 teeth which is more than any other mammal in North America.

Turkey Vulture
A turkey vulture can vomit up to 10 feet when it gets scared. It has the largest smelling system of all birds. Turkey Vultures love to eat smelly dead animals.

Printed in the United States
by Baker & Taylor Publisher Services